The Valley of the FROST GIANTS

Lothrop, Lee & Shepard Company, New York

The Valley of the FROST GIANTS

Mary Francis Shura

Illustrated by Charles Keeping

To Kier of Thirty Acres

Contents

1
The Bird

So many ships had gone from this place and so few had returned that the high white cliff was named Farewell. The top of the cliff was secreted in clouds, and its base was hollowed with caves by the sea that had thundered against it since the very beginning.

Around the cliff and into the valley beyond, blue mist curled from the sea and circled the cottage of the Viking who lived there among his fields with his wife and two children, Rolf and Freia.

His son Rolf was as straight and strong as a mighty spear, and his daughter Freia as golden and graceful as

a shaft of wheat. The Viking looked on them with pride and love as he told them good-bye.

"But why must you go from us?" Freia asked, looking up through the thick foam of her father's beard to where his eyes shone as brightly blue as the very sea of morning.

His laughter rumbled about the cottage.

"Because I am a man and a Viking, and there is a world beyond the waves that I must see."

"But what if you do not return?" she asked softly, hushed by her own fear.

"I will have done what I had to do," he said gently. Then he kissed her upon her forehead and laid a hand very hard on Rolf's shoulder and strode swiftly through the blue mist to where his ship fretted against its anchor.

Together with their mother, Rolf and Freia stood on the high white cliff to watch him go. They watched the even sweep of the oars as the ship sped toward the sunset. To bring good fortune they waved and waved until the sails were no longer a speck, not even the memory of a speck.

Then together they went down the mountain into the Blue Valley of home.

Spring turned to summer, and Rolf and Freia planted the seed that their father had left, that there might be bread against the long winter.

Freia startled the small hares from the brush, and Rolf caught them, that there might be dried meat against the dark winter.

Freia and Mother stitched together the skins of the deer that Father had left, that there might be warm clothes against the cold winter.

Summer turned toward autumn. The grain stirred gently in the soft blue air, and pale stars shone.

"When can we harvest our grain, Mother?" Rolf asked. Already his breath curled mist about his mouth when he spoke at twilight.

His mother frowned. "If the good days number seven, our grain will be ripe for harvest." She looked fearfully at the darkening sky as if she feared that the Frost Giants were listening from behind the high white cliff.

Her fear was well founded. The good days numbered only six. The Frost Giants swept their scythes through the Blue Valley, and the grain fell darkly.

Through that long winter there was no bread. Mother became slender, as lean as a birch tree. When spring rose from the earth in soft flowers, Mother, Freia, and Rolf rejoiced together.

"Can we plant again?" Rolf asked. "Can we find seed?"

Mother smiled. She showed him a secret place, and in it the small sack of seed grain she had kept hidden through the long winter.

Rolf and Freia readied the soil. As Mother was bringing the bag of seeds for them to plant, a shadow fell on her. Wider than the valley the broad wings swept, darker than the longest night of winter were the feathers of the great black bird's breast.

The bird seized Mother's bag of seeds in his great bill and tugged.

How stoutly Mother screamed in protest; how stubbornly she clung to her precious seed. Rolf and Freia ran quickly to help her. Rolf caught hold of his mother even as she started to rise into the air, and Freia seized him about the waist.

Higher, higher and higher they rose until the plowed earth was a dark square far below them. Over the cliff the great bird flew, still holding the bag of grain.

Rolf looked down at the mountains, and at the fiords, and at the sea whipped white against the stones. He could bear to look no more. He only held as tightly to his mother as Freia clung to him. He could hear Freia weeping with fright. She was a girl. She could cry. He tightened his lips against the stinging wind, and closed his eyes.

So thin was Mother from the winter without bread that her apron began to slip. Although Rolf held on as tightly as he could, he felt his mother slipping from him. Rolf fell with Freia still clinging to him. The big bird flew on, carrying Mother and the bag of seed into a bank of clouds.

Down and *down* and *down* they fell. Dizzily Rolf watched the world turn and spin. Surely they would strike the stones along the sea's edge and be dashed to nothing.

Giddy with fright, Rolf kept his eyes closed and waited for the wild plunge to be over.

2
The Baby

There came a sudden thud. To Rolf's surprise, he felt himself springing into the air again and again before coming to rest. Beside him, he heard Freia's small gasps of amazement.

Opening his eyes, Rolf stared about. Only a few feet away was the white frothed sea. Only a few feet beneath him rose the jagged teeth of the craggy rocks. But he and Freia swayed gently in a great net suspended between two large stones.

Freia too was staring about, her eyes large with fear as she caught at Rolf's hand.

They looked about to see the owner of the net they had fallen into. They listened tensely, but could only hear the sweep of sea and the moan of wind among the caves.

"Whose net is this?" Freia whispered softly, as if the stones were listening.

"I do not know," Rolf replied softly. "But it has saved our lives."

As they spoke, a soft strange sound began somewhere in one of the caves that ringed the beach. Though soft and muted, it was the unmistakable cry of a baby.

Rolf helped Freia scramble from the net, and they followed the sound. Inside the dimness they found the child. Now he was crying fiercely, shaking his fists and kicking his tiny legs wildly.

"You poor thing, you poor baby," Freia cried. She ran to the child and lifted him from his hammock of dried seaweed. His mouth puckered into a small pout as he tucked his head in contented silence against her shoulder.

"Why would a baby be in this wild place?" Rolf wondered aloud as he looked at the baby nestling against Freia.

The mouth of the cave suddenly darkened.

Rolf whirled around.

In the doorway, blocking the sun, stood two small

men. Dwarfs they must be, Rolf decided quickly. They were knobby of head, and their arms bulged with muscles of great strength.

"Hail," Rolf said, recovering from his surprise. "Was that your net that saved our lives?"

The dwarf nodded solemnly.

"To you we owe great thanks," Rolf told him. "For though the net is soft and silken as a ribbon, it held us safely from the stones."

"I hope we did no damage to your net," Freia said softly.

"In truth, the net cannot be put to a test," the dwarf replied. "It was fashioned by certain dwarfs in the region of the Black Elves . . .

> *From the noise a cat makes when its foot falls.*
> *From the beard of a woman.*
> *From the roots of a rock.*
> *From the sinews of a bear.*
> *From the spittle of a bird."*

"But surely those things are not to be found," Rolf said.

The dwarf nodded again. "For that reason they cannot be put to the test."

They stood a moment in silence. Then the dwarf spoke again.

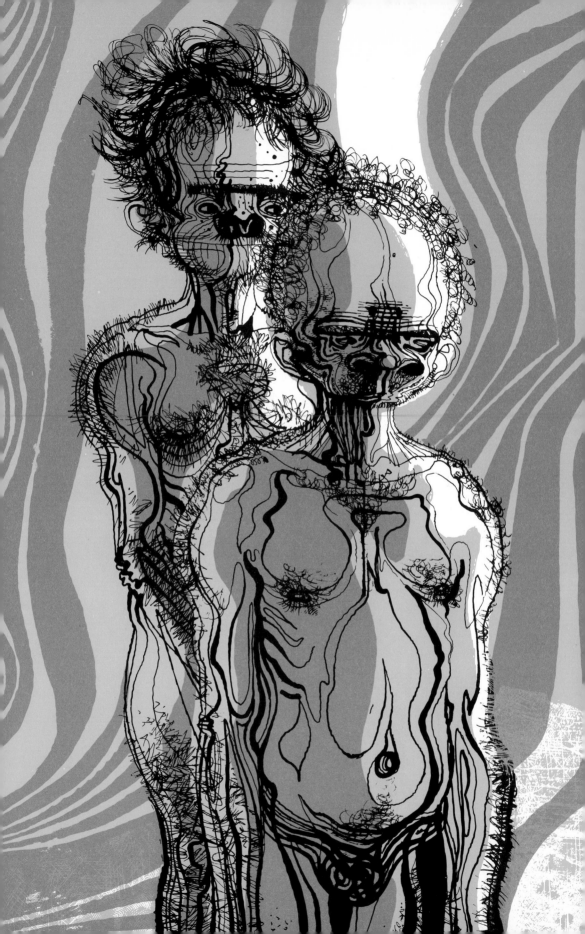

"The child you are holding also fell into the net. A black bird as wide as the sky hurled him here. But we can find no peace for him. He only lies and cries."

"Perhaps he is hungry," Freia suggested.

"He accepts no food that we offer," the dwarf explained.

Freia swayed back and forth, rocking the sleeping baby.

"Let my brother and me take care of him," she asked, "to repay you for our lives."

"So it shall be," the dwarf replied. Still without smiling, he nodded solemnly at the children and backed from the cave, leaving Freia and Rolf alone with their charge.

Rolf looked at the child questioningly. "You may have chosen a difficult thing to do," he suggested to Freia, who was crooning happily.

"Not so much," she protested. "We'll feed him and bathe him, and soon he'll be a child like ourselves." Then she frowned. "But how shall we get him home?"

"Home!" cried Rolf. "We cannot leave this place. For one thing, we do not know where the Blue Valley lies from here. And for another, if our mother should escape that great bird she would come here, searching for us."

Freia agreed. When she and Rolf walked forth from the cave, the dwarfs were gone. The glistening net no longer swung between its stones, and the beach was empty of marks of their going.

With branches that he gathered along the beach, Rolf built a small lean-to beyond the last tongue of the tide, in a curve of sheltering stones.

When it was finished, Freia smiled and sat in that homely place, rocking the sleeping child gently in her arms.

"When he wakens, he will be hungry," she whispered to her brother.

"I have thought of that," Rolf nodded. "When I was gathering branches I saw pale smoke from beyond the hill. I shall go there for help."

Leaving the child with Freia, Rolf took the path across the beach and over the hill. He was at once gone from sight.

3
The Wise Woman

Rolf followed the small wavering of smoke and soon—at a sudden bend—came upon a cottage. On the eaves of the cottage, a sheaf of grain had been hung. A company of small birds was feeding there and singing bright songs of gratitude.

"Who lives in this house is kindly," Rolf told himself.

As he neared the door, Rolf saw neat rows of wood against the house, cutting the breath of the north wind from its walls.

"Who lives in this house is wise," he told himself.

When the door was opened to him, the woman looked not only kindly, but very very old.

When they had exchanged greetings, Rolf spoke of the child.

"My sister and I have a foundling," he told the old woman. "Can you tell me where I can buy milk with my labor?"

"What kind of a foundling?" the old woman asked.

"A boy child who fell into the net of the dwarfs," Rolf explained.

The old woman nodded her head. "If he is the child of earth people, he will drink the milk of a reindeer. If he is not . . . ," she shrugged and turned away.

When she returned, she carried a fluted shell quite filled with reindeer milk, which she handed to Rolf.

"Thank you, good woman," Rolf said. "May I pay you?"

"Wait to see if the baby drinks it," the woman told him.

Freia set the shell on a sun-warmed rock. Soon the baby stirred to wakefulness. Freia held the shell to the baby's lips, and he tasted the rich golden milk. He made a great face and began to cry again, flailing his fists so that the shell was nearly overturned.

"You drink the milk, sister," Rolf suggested. "And I will return the shell to the old woman."

When he told the woman what had happened, she nodded wisely.

"The foundling is not of our kind," she told Rolf. "If you were wise, you would hurl him into the sea."

"Oh, but I cannot," Rolf protested.

"Why not?" the old woman asked.

"Because I am the son of a Viking, and I choose to be a friend to the weak."

The old woman shrugged. "So it must be, then. If it is the child of dwarfs, it will eat the eggs of the sea tern."

"Thank you," he told her.

"And if that does not work, you might come again," she called after him.

Rolf searched among the rocks of the shoreline until his feet were sore. It was cold and dark when Rolf finally returned to Freia with three tern eggs cupped carefully in his hands.

Over a little fire of driftwood, they warmed the eggs. The baby opened his mouth like a bird, and took one bite. Then he spat the egg out, yelling fiercely. Freia had to hold him tightly lest he fall.

"Eat the warm eggs, brother," Freia insisted. "You will need strength to search again."

At dawn, Rolf rose and made his way to the cottage of the old woman.

"He would not eat the egg of the tern?" she asked, looking at Rolf's face.

He nodded.

"If you are wise, you will throw him into the sea now," she warned.

"Oh, but I cannot," Rolf replied.

She looked at him and sighed. "If he is the child of giants, there is only one food he will eat," she warned.

"And what is that?" Rolf asked, a small fear beginning to form beneath his ribs.

The old woman came from her house, walking painfully on a bent stick. Bracing herself on her cane, she turned to the north and pointed her finger high, waving it as she spoke.

"Beyond that hill and the next and the third, there stretches a great green pasture. In that pasture grazes one great cow. Her horns are curled trumpets, and her hooves are like unsheathed swords. Her gaze is swifter than eagles."

Rolf waited a long time before the old woman spoke again.

"That cow," she said slowly, "is the milk cow of the giants. If they should discover that you steal milk from them, you would never return."

"I shall have to take that chance," Rolf decided aloud.

The old woman shrugged, and made her way back

to her cottage. She returned and handed Rolf a small leather pouch.

"You will need something in which to carry the milk," she explained. "Luck go with you."

Rolf looked toward the glowing north. Should he go back and tell Freia where he was going? He decided not to waste that time. He started north to seek the cow, reminding himself over and again that he was the son of a Viking and must have courage for all tasks.

4

The Cow of the Giants

For what seemed a long time, Rolf walked briskly with the leather pouch swinging at his side. He journeyed to the hill beyond the hill, then stopped to rest before going on.

The grass where Rolf sat was thickly tufted with sweet-smelling flowers. As he rose to continue his journey, he plucked a handful of blossoms and tucked them inside his coat.

When Rolf reached the crest of the third hill, he could see for a great distance. The great green pasture was just as the old woman had described it. As he began

to walk toward it Rolf noticed, in the grass at his feet, the dried spine of a fish. The bones of the fish were so white and strong that Rolf turned the skeleton in his hand in wonder before putting it inside his coat, along with the flowers.

A silence seemed to fall about Rolf as he first stepped into the pasture. There was not even the hum of an insect, nor the call of a bird. The grass moved about his legs with a hushed whisper. The great cow, her horns gleaming like golden trumpets, stood silently and stared at him as he drew near.

Rolf almost held his breath, so fearful he was that he might startle her into flight. Only when he was quite near, did he carefully pull the flowers from inside his coat and hold them out to her.

The cow stared at the flowers, at Rolf, and then looked all about cautiously. When she turned back to Rolf, she approached him, and ate the flowers from his hand.

Rolf drew from his coat the fish spine. The cow sniffed it questioningly. Then Rolf scratched her, first on her nose, then between her ears, and finally along the wide lane of her spine. Her eyes were half shut with pleasure as the boy groomed her. Finally, she laid her head against his shoulder.

Rolf took out the leather pouch. The cow stood quietly to let him fill the pouch with her milk. Rolf

closed the pouch and swung it from his shoulder.

"Good creature, gentle cow," he told her. He felt her stiffen beneath his hand. Looking across the wide meadow, he saw something coming in the distance.

Wildly, Rolf turned to flee toward the ocean, where Freia waited.

But the giant had seen him. The giant's voice rolled along the hills like thunder. Rolf dared not look back. He ran on swiftly. Behind him he heard the winding of a terrible trumpet. He felt the earth beneath him shake with the thunder of many giants' feet. Rolf only ran harder, not looking back.

But even as his heart ached against his ribs, he wondered which giants these might be.

Were they the Hill Giants, who could tumble the mountains with a huge earthquake? Were they the Fire Giants, who would blaze him in his path with bolts of lightning?

The air grew chill. Snow began to fall from the clear sky. Rolf knew that his pursuers must be the Frost Giants, who crushed whole villages beneath their avalanches and trapped Viking ships in frozen seas.

The giants gained on Rolf steadily, and the breath of their shouts froze the air before them. The old woman's cottage was glazed with ice as Rolf passed. Freia was waiting, shivering in the small shelter, holding the crying baby very close to her for warmth.

Pulling the pouch open with half-frozen fingers, Rolf fed the baby.

The infant drank and drank.

The earth about them trembled from the nearness of the gaints. Freia suddenly cried out. The child was growing. By the time the pouch was one-fourth empty, the child was taller than Freia herself. Freia wept with fright.

The baby seized the pouch and stood erect, holding the pouch to his own lips and continuing to drink. By the time the pouch was halfway empty, the child was taller than the woman's cottage.

Rolf and Freia, watching, cringed against the rocks. Then the baby was full grown. His head towered above the hills as he turned to face the Frost Giants who stalked down the beach, swirling storms about their angry feet.

Rolf held Freia closely, terrified.

5
The Giants

"Hail, brothers," the baby cried joyfully as the giants approached.

The Frost Giants halted their advance. They stood silently a moment, staring at the child before seizing him with shouts of affection. They would have borne him off without hesitation; but the baby leaned down and scooped up Rolf and Freia in one hand. Together the giants strode off across the hills to the home of their father.

"Father, our lost brother is found." The Frost Giants vied in shouting the good news across the frozen hills in their voices of thunder.

The old giant roared with happiness. He took Rolf and Freia into his own hand and set them upon one of his vast fingernails. His huge face drew very near as he squinted closely at them.

"Tell me how this came to be, that such small, helpless creatures as you could bring me my son?"

Rolf told the Frost Giant of the great black bird that had tried to steal the seed grain from Mother, of his and Freia's flight, and their fall.

The giant nodded as Rolf spoke. "Bird he may seem to be," he said. "But, in truth, he is a spirit of mischief who travels about in that form. That same black bird seized my child. But that is over." His voice rose with happiness. "My son is returned, and we may all rejoice together."

"We are together, Father," the young giant reminded him. "But what of these children, of their parents, and their home?"

"Of course, of course," the old giant shouted. "Forgive my thoughtless joy. Where is your mother? Where is your home?"

"Our home is in the Blue Valley," Rolf replied. "But of our mother we cannot say. She was in the clutch of the black bird when we saw her last."

One of the Frost Giants nodded quickly. "I know the valley well. One white rock named Farewell stands there against the sea."

"And I know the nest of the black bird," his brother said. "I will seek your mother in that hiding place."

Swifter than cold winds ever moved before, they swept the children home to their Blue Valley. The door swung open on their cottage twice. The third time, a gale blew their mother in, gasping with fear, and quite blue with cold, but still gripping the bag of seed grain.

Before the Frost Giants left, Rolf handed them the fish spine to groom the cow. The old giant shook his great head, a dark cloud hanging over his icy face.

"You shame us with your goodness. What kindness could we do in return?"

When Rolf did not at once reply, Freia spoke softly.

"If our grain fields were never to feel your touch until the seed is ripened, we would be grateful beyond all dreams."

"This wish will come to pass," the Frost Giant said simply. He held the broad palm of his hand one moment above the Blue Valley, and then the Frost Giants went away, leaving only Rolf and Freia and their mother beside the cottage in the fields.

Rolf and Freia planted the seed in the Blue Valley. The warm rains and gentle sun and the friendship of the Frost Giants brought it to harvest.

One day, Rolf and Freia were walking along the white cliff named Farewell. They saw, on the very edge

of the world, the color of sails. Breathlessly they watched the ship come near—near enough that they could see their own father standing as tall as a second mast, his beard like a banner blowing in the wind of the sea.

The valley echoed with shouts of joy as their father, the Viking, strode with them through the fields to his cottage.

"Ah," he sighed, as he warmed his feet at his own fire, "to be at home again. I bring great tales to tell you, of red men and white waves and giant storms."

"And we have great tales to tell you, Father," Rolf replied, "of Mother flying above the earth, and Freia nursing a giant. . . ."

"Hold! Hold!" the father cried in amazement. "What is it that you have done?"

"We are the children of a Viking," Rolf reminded him. "And we have done what things there were to do."

Ever thereafter plenty joined peace in the cottage of the Viking in the Blue Valley behind the white cliff. Farewell.

1 2 3 4 5 75 74 73 72 71